The Dream To End All Dreams

Rebecca Ryder

For Shelby

CHAPTER 1

Mr Henderson left behind two things. The first was his body. The second, a handwritten note tucked into the folds of his hospital gown. A note that made him the most remarkable patient I had ever cared for.

At 29, Mr Henderson was only a few years older than me. It was rare that I got to look after someone so young and it was always sad, but as with every hospital job, a certain amount of death was to be expected. As a nurse, I never felt close to death myself, but I knew it better than anyone else. I sat with it every day, stroking its hand, chatting to it, even laughing with it. Yet, I never quite understood it. It was as if death had employed me as its secretary, and as such, a certain level of respect was to be given.

I cannot begin to tell you how awful it is, watching someone come to terms with the inevitable. Death is cruel, so cruel that even just its presence causes suffering. The constant anxiety, sadness and irritability, knowing that nothing will last forever. That all the things we do, make, and achieve, will vanish or be forgotten, including us. All this from the quiet, miserable, senseless neighbour that often visits when we least expect it.

Patients often looked up to me for answers. Sometimes pleading and begging as if I held the secrets to the universe in the palm of my hands. I did not.

The morning of Mr Henderson's death, I went to check his blood pressure. While doing so, another nurse popped in, breaking the news that his family had phoned. We had informed them of Mr Henderson's deteriorating condition, but their travel plans had been delayed and we were doubtful they would make it on time.

"Why don't you get some rest?" I said to Mr Henderson. "You'll need your energy when your family comes to visit you."

"I can't sleep when I know I might never wake again." he replied.

Moving a chair next to his bed, I sat and reassured him. What was supposed to be a quick check-in before my break, turned into an hour-long conversation. He told me about his life, his worries, his troubles, his hopes and his dreams. I tried to answer his questions, and he tried to answer mine.

That afternoon, I went over to the side of his bed to check his vitals. It was then that he opened his eyes, and with a gasp of breath, grabbed my hand. I held onto him, watching his pupils explode, engulfing his eyes with darkness. In less than a minute, his grip on my hand loosened, his chest deflated, and he lay still. He was gone.

I returned to his room that evening to log the time and date of his departure. I stood in front of the stranger again. Now that I saw him in a lifeless state, I noticed that there was no change in the world around him after he had gone. Babies were being born on the floor above, their cries of life breaking off and floating down through the open window. Outside, trains still whizzed on by, the passengers oblivious to the tragic events that unfolded here every day. People in the next room laughed. Life went on. Life went on and the world continued to turn.

Moving towards him, I lifted the edge of the drape to check the patient number on his wrist. It was then that I saw the note, tucked into the folds of his hospital gown. I picked it up and opened it.

To Sophie and Jack,

If you are reading this, it is because I have passed away.

It hurts me to think how much pain you must be in right now. I don't expect this letter to help much, but I would be stupid if I did not try.

The truth is, you will forever be known as the children whose father died an alcoholic and addict. When you see other families, you'll question why they have a father. You will find yourself asking; "Why did my dad have to die?", "Is my life over?"

Your life is not over, perhaps it is on hold, but it's not over. You will be all right, I have no doubt of that. Not now, maybe not for a while, but believe me, you will be alright.

I know you'll often think about the last morning we opened presents together, our final day out at the park, the night I carried you to bed for the last time. I hope that eventually, you can think of these moments with a smile.

I won't be around to see you grow up. For that, I am sorry. I'm sure you'll wish I could be there to hug you when you fall out with your friends, to cheer and clap loudly when you graduate, to help fix your car when it breaks down and to walk you down the aisle on your wedding day.

I may not be there physically, but please know that I am rooting you on and I am proud of you.

You have given me so much joy. I hope your heart will fill you with the desire to go on to live a wonderful life. Love each other and make me proud. If you miss a day, it doesn't matter. There will always be the next. I know that tomorrow morning, you will rise again, as will the sun.

One of the most wonderful privileges in life is the chance to say goodbye. I'm so sorry I missed mine.

In the past months I have spent in and out of hospital, I have been lucky enough to be treated with such kindness. I never knew this much love was possible from strangers.

As I lie here, please know that my mind is filled with our memories, from your cheeky laughs to your sprawling tears and everything that fits between.

I will miss you both greatly, and I hope we can be together again. Thank you for bringing more joy into my life than I could have ever imagined.

Until we meet again,
love,

Dad xx

You might think that his death had nothing to do with me, and you'd be right. But I couldn't help but feel otherwise. Being surrounded by death, I was constantly reminded of the fragility of life. During our last conversation, he said numerous times, "Jonathan, I made the mistake of thinking I had time.", he told me how he wished he had more of it.

Many of the people I looked after said similarly, and I often left work feeling that I wasn't living dangerously enough to justify the time I'd been given. But on the day Mr Henderson died, not only did I feel guilty for being alive, I felt guilty for not changing the inevitable.

As I wrote down the date and time of Mr Henderson's departure, I felt particularly empty. The passage of time had always made me nauseous, but his letter was the one thing that really stuck with me. No matter how many times I did this, I never got used to it. Strange to think that the same life that is so full of wisdom, happiness and love can be condensed into nothing more than a brief dash between two dates.

Later, I had a quiet cry in the staff room, the waves of emotion slipping forth now they were no longer restrained. Two nurses heard my whimpers and came over to comfort me.

"If you're going to cry this much, perhaps you should rethink your career?" she said.

The head nurse replied, "Darling, if there ever comes a time you don't cry, that's when you need to stop being a nurse."

They did not know I was also crying for me.

That evening, I gathered up my belongings and clocked out, the fluorescent lights flickering down the corridor behind me. Whenever I left work, I could never tell if I was walking towards something or walking away. All I knew was that I wanted to help others and had rent to pay. Apart from that, I had no desire to be there, but I had no desire to leave. It was just something I accepted as part of my conditions for living.

Stepping outside through the doors, I felt the cool evening breeze brush over my face. I turned and began my walk down the hill towards the car park. As I approached my car, a familiar-looking scene caught my attention. The sun had disappeared behind the hill and the sky had faded to violet hues. This once common sight of my childhood had now become a simple reminder to me. A reminder of the past. What I could have done, what I should've done and what I could've been. I often wondered if I was wrong to honour the memory of the days that had slipped on by. After all, the body of today had fallen, but it was still breathing. Was I wrong to mourn something still alive?

These thoughts appeared too often to maintain a feeling of normality. You see, being a human didn't come naturally to me the way it seemed to for others. I made the mistake of trying to understand the world before I could understand myself, and soon enough, I fell victim to my hopes and ambitions. The only thing I had created was an alternate reality, a sort of retreat, a place of escape. A world where I had everything I desired and became everything I aspired to be—

handsome, witty, smart and successful. But the irony was, I suffered there too, sometimes even more than reality.

For perhaps a minute I stayed there, mourning the sun. My gaze kept pulling toward the alley in front of me, at the end of which sat The Barge Inn. I was close enough that I could see the dark wooden sign swaying gently above the entrance. Pacing towards it, the glow from its windows was felt as it spilled out onto the narrow pavement. It was a place I knew well, a place that I often called home.

The door swung shut behind me with a muffled thud, sealing off the outside world. I stood there a moment, feeling the transition from cold street to enclosed atmosphere. The air inside seemed heavier, as if everyone carried a burden, unseen, unspoken, but felt by all. This was a temporary escape from the harsh realities waiting outside.

I moved forward, the low murmur of conversations surrounding me. A shared feeling of loneliness that fuelled the illusion of camaraderie. In this little murky bar, the demons within us were laid bare and the boundaries between perpetrator and victim, abandoner and abandoned, blurred into dissonant harmony.

The barstools were all occupied by silhouettes, each nursing their own shadows with a drink in hand. I found a seat opposite, the worn leather creaking beneath me as I settled in. My favourite bartender acknowledged my presence with a nod. I signalled back to him, the unspoken understanding between us cutting through the noise. Soon enough, a glass appeared before me, amber liquid glinting in the dim light.

To numb the pain within, I had sought solace in the bottom of a bottle. A temporary escape, a feeling of reprieve from the relentless barrage of self-doubt. Leaning back in my chair, the edge of the glass touching my lips, I braced myself for the first wonderful sip. It did not disappoint. The world still tasted bitter but at last, my demons went silent.

Seven in one evening, that had to be some kind of record. After a brief moment of hesitation, I let my regrets go. After all, maybe things weren't that bad. At least here in this bar, I had hope, a false illusion of normality. It was not the first time I found myself in this position, but it was the last.

A bartender came over, collecting my glasses. "Everything alright?" he muttered.

"No. I'm not okay. There's an ache in my stomach that hasn't stopped for weeks. I'm constantly tired, unwell and sick. Why do we allow ourselves to suffer? I've been asking that question a lot lately. The thoughts and feelings I have are overwhelming. Blurred memories, clouded visions, unable to tell fiction from fantasy. Oh, such a beautiful disaster the mind is. My problem is, I care. I always care. I devote my life to helping people, yet I wonder why I've never taken the time to help myself. Knowing is a curse sometimes, yet I still seek answers. Who am I? Why am I here? What's the point of it all? Why do I put myself through this pain? These questions are always floating about. I have no answers. None at all."

But I didn't say that, I didn't say anything at all. Why? Well, sometimes the facts are better left unspoken. It can be so unpleasant to tell the truth when the result is your own humiliation. People often forget that.

The truth was, I had fallen deep inside the crevice of thoughts that ran within my mind. I tried to focus on the light above but instead, only felt the walls around me squeezing tightly, a constant reminder that I was somewhere I was not supposed to be. The occasional person walked on by above, never noticing me. If they did, they did not dare to say anything.

I often felt these emotions were unnecessary. After all, I had quite a few acquaintances just inside those hospital doors, fifty yards away, up the stairs and across the hallway. There were at least a handful of people working there that I would call friends. Yet I would not admit my feelings to any of them, as it would've only made me look weak.

This was not an emotion I ever shared openly with anyone. Depression is a dirty word. Some people have probably never felt it, they're the lucky ones. It's a feeling of emptiness, of nothing. How would you describe nothing? You can't. It's like describing sight to the blind. Music to the deaf.

I looked down into my half-empty glass and pondered. I had kept asking questions and searching for answers, but God did not respond. I looked up, just in case he was listening, but was met with the familiar ceiling, painted like white meringue. I tried numerous times to reach out with my atheist hand. To embrace a source of hope, a half answer to my half questions. There was never any answer. To think that this God knows me better than I know myself, stays silent in times of need, refuses to cure my suffering, to answer my questions, but would not hesitate to send me to hell for simply not believing, does not suggest that he is good. If such a God existed, he was no God of mine.

After finishing my drink, I stumbled out the door, my feet carrying me towards my car. I fumbled for the keys in my hands, the jingling piercing through the rain. The one working streetlight did its best, but everything was a blur of shadows and silhouettes. Eventually, the door opened and I stumbled into the driving seat.

As I eased out onto the road, the hum of the engine rose as the wheels met the open street. Music came over the radio and as I picked up speed, the cool autumn wind began whipping down through the sunroof against my face. I smiled. For at that fleeting moment, all my worries and disillusionments were cast across the road in front of me, bathed in my amber lights.

On nights like these, there was no speed limit. Only a few miles away from home and I accelerated into the dip before the hill, following the white line as it leaned right. Gentle with the throttle as the road twisted back left. Off the throttle as I emerged over the hill, snaking on through. Slight left and a dip down by the golf course— my signal to accelerate. Faster and faster, the rain on the window flying upwards, my chest sinking into my seat.

The lines on the road danced, mocking my impaired senses. Thoughts collided in my mind, a chaotic symphony of regret. I struggled to take control, teetering on the edge of disaster. Then, like a fleeting moment in time, it happened.

A screech of tyres, a blinding flash, and the sickening sound of metal crashing against metal. At that moment, time stood still. My thoughts suspended from me as my consciousness drifted between the lines of nothingness. The weight of my choices and the consequences of my actions converged in that singular, haunting moment. Regret surged through my veins, mingling with the bitter taste of alcohol on my tongue.

Time slammed back into its normal rhythm. My mind replaced by the hazy glow of consciousness. I soon found myself trapped within a new reality. Pain seared through my body, a visceral reminder of the wreckage I had caused. The wreckage of my car, the wreckage of my life.

The world around me came back into focus, the chaos of the accident unfolding before my eyes. The gusts of wind carried the screams of innocent victims. In the distance, sirens wailed, a strange orchestra of chaos. The echoes of the accident reverberated in my mind, an unwelcome reminder of the fragility of it all. At that moment, there was no escaping the consequences of my actions. The price of my despair had been paid in broken glass and twisted metal.

People rushed around me, their faces filled with concern. Shaken passersby walked amongst the wreckage, their shouts distant and muffled. But through it all, a single thought resounded within me: I had hit rock bottom, both figuratively and literally.

I clung to the fraying threads of consciousness, but they slipped through my fingers like grains of sand. As the excruciating pain pounded from within my chest, I finally surrendered to the darkness, watching curtains close, and everything fade to black.

CHAPTER 2

As I crossed the border of consciousness, I found myself floating, weightless and perfect. I must have been there for less than a second, but I felt that the distance between myself and my body was the greatest it had ever been.

Thinking I was about to die, I braced for the end. But then, I felt it— a single drop of water kissed my cheek, its cool surface sending a tingle of sweet energy travelling through every inch of my body. I wasn't dead, not yet anyway.

I reached out to steady myself, only to find my fingertips dancing between blades of grass. I took a deep breath, letting the smell of earthy soil blanket over me with a gentle breeze.

I opened my eyes and was welcomed by the bright blue sky looking back at me. Looking down over my chest I watched as an emerald landscape unfolded between my feet. Green rolling hills stretched out like brushstrokes on canvas, clusters of trees dotted across each peak. In the distance, a carpet of flowers majestically greeted my eyes. To the left, a vast expanse of land where the sea shook hands with the earth, stretched on endlessly. For a moment, I wondered if I had woken up in paradise.

As I got up from the ground, I noticed the strangeness in the landscape in front of me. The sky was blue, the birds were singing and everything was wrong. I couldn't remember how I got there, but I knew something didn't belong. By now a sense of confusion and panic was beginning to develop. Where was I? What was I doing here? I stood out as a lone silhouette, a drop of black ink on a canvas filled with colour. Where was everyone else?

I was still getting to know the panorama before me when the rain tapped at my shoulders. As I turned around, a storm introduced itself to me from a distance. Without warning, it began to move forward, parting the blue sky as it rolled towards me. Other clouds began to move in fast, the vibrant colours draining around me as the darkness enveloped my vision. The wind was getting colder and the rain tapping harder. I was lost. A feeling I was used to, but here it was particularly present. There was nowhere I wanted to go, but I couldn't stay here.

It was then that I noticed a well-trodden dirt path that wrapped itself around the trees in front of me. Before I could even think so much as a thought, I already found my feet dragging myself towards it. As I walked, the world around me seemed to blur, the colours bleeding into one another like watercolours on canvas. I thought I was moving but I felt as though I was simply getting smaller and smaller.

After what felt like an eternity of walking, I noticed the trail forked up ahead into two diverging routes. I slowed to a stop, my chest tightening with a creeping sense of dread. A decision point, and with no clear guidance on which way to go.

Pivoting on my heel, I searched the green landscape for any sign or clues to orientate myself. That's when I spotted something in the overgrowth. Pushing through the bushes, a large wooden sign came into focus, with paint obscuring the information. Rather than giving answers, it held a single inscrutable phrase painted in bold red strokes "You are here now."

I gazed down each fork, searching for clues, some visible difference revealing the right direction. The storm growled behind me, but I still had no answers. The sign, with its message, a philosophical riddle I grasped at futilely, like trying to catch smoke between my fingers. I was here now, though where 'here' was remained a mystery.

By this time rain had begun to march against the soil around me. I was soaked to the core, all my energy draining from within. I was tired of running away from everything and as my desperation began to build, I dug my nails into the letters and picked furiously. Paint chipped away until it uncovered a map beneath. There, in simple clarity, were the two diverging paths. Nothing else. No answers. Just a choice, a pond or a church.

I had always turned my back on the idea that religion could help, but considering my circumstances, it seemed to be the more sensible option of the two.

Following the path to the right, my steps quickened, trying desperately to stay ahead of the storm. I followed the path around through the winding trees and up a slight incline until the church spire took shape against the bruised sky. As I drew nearer, I could make out the graveyard surrounding it. Row upon row of weather-worn headstones fanning out like a petrified congregation. An apprehensive chill lashed my spine, but I pressed onwards until I pushed through the rusting gate.

My footsteps felt leaden, each one taking a great effort to move through the damp earth. As I slowly made my way along one of the rows, something made me pause and stare harder at a particular headstone jutting crookedly from the ground ahead. My fingers moved over the name, my heart seizing as I recognised it:

HENDERSON

My breath flew away, separating itself from the confines of my lungs. I felt the world tilt violently, sending my knees buckling as I staggered forward and hit the ground. But as my blurred vision scanned the surrounding plots, a sickening realisation took hold - I recognized every single name. All of them being patients I had attended to over the years. Men, women, children. All those lives I had brushed up against, all ultimately leading to this graveyard.

I clawed at the ground, my mind spinning with sickness. Guilt. I tried frequently to rid myself of such feelings, but my hands kept picking it up and pouring it over my brow when all was silent. My soul ached for the deaths I accompanied, and as if caring wasn't enough, I had formed the habit of feeling responsible.

Those feelings were soon accompanied by the rage and despair that churned within my gut. Any hope I had was now anger. I was no longer just observing death, I was experiencing it. It provided no answers. What twisted joke was this? To find myself transported to this beautiful world, only to be confronted by a sprawling memorial to my life's failures?

How could I have been so arrogant, so delusional as to think this place could provide hope? This entire desolate expanse was the personification of my life's most profound inadequacies. I was surrounded by the ghosts of those I could not help, despite my greatest mortal strivings.

Shaking with a combination of grief and rage, I stormed up the path and threw myself against the arched doors, forcing my way inside. If this place held any answers, any secrets to unlocking the existential mysteries that had gnawed at me for so long, I would beat them out of its very foundations.

The doors groaned in protest as I threw my weight against them once again. On the third attempt, they finally gave way, swinging wide to reveal the vaulted interior beyond.

Despite the circumstances that had led me here, there was an undeniable aura of peace and sanctuary suffusing the ancient stone walls. For a moment, I was struck by the peacefulness of the place. Rows of wooden pews led up to a platform at the front, with colourful illustrations in the stained glass either side.

"Please," I pleaded, my voice barely more than a whisper. "show me that I'm not alone. Show me there is still hope."

The silence that greeted me was deafening.

I thought of all those people who lay outside, those patients who perished seeking answers to questions I could never answer. Maybe here, I could finally voice those questions, on behalf of those who never got the chance. My message to God began as a lump in my throat, but I knew that if I wanted any form of answer, I would have to speak out loud, to make my voice known, to search for the answer rather than to expect it.

My frustration reached a crescendo, accompanying me as I moved down the aisle towards the altar.

"I have been on this earth for over a quarter of a century, and I have seen life as it really is. I have held patients as their world collapsed around them. I have heard them singing their prayers and shouting to God. Some found peace in believing, and for that, I thank you. Yet, so many died with panic, pain and a general sense of uncertainty. They asked questions for which I had no answers, and I often made the mistake of telling the truth. For is it not cruel to mock our understanding of reality? To create illusions that warp the line between life and death? I walk that line to guide those unwilling to cross it. To make the unknown slightly easier to understand, to make the unbearable slightly more pleasant. The people who lay out there. They are people who once had hope, and they are people who eventually saw life as it is. I don't blame them, I know all too well that when life throws us problems we cannot solve, we look for hope. When so many of our questions are met with silence, we take our answers where we can. Some of those people hoped that one day I would find God. I found God, more than once. I found God looking at my reflection on the blade of a razor. I found God in a bottle of whiskey. Those are my

Gods. Why? No other God listened. You gave us the tools to confront a reality so bleak, that we evolved to create tools to deny it ourselves. I have watched loved ones fade away, only to be bought back in the name of God. I have watched family members beg us to simply keep their loved one alive, to stave off the inevitable ending we all insist on defying. These were moments of desperation, choices taken under the influence of faith, blinded by reality. This is the illusion of hope. The double-edged sword that lives and breathes amongst us. Hope is irrational. Hope is a disease that mutates, evolves, and spreads between humans. It is fuelled by the curse that is consciousness, and when it becomes an optimistic delusion, it is the very last thing to leave the body. I was never caring for these people. I tortured them with every turn, dressing change, bath. I created hell on earth. This is unnecessary. Living shouldn't be a burden, but if it is, the choice to end our lives should be acknowledged. We children of yours. We fight for hope, we fight for answers, we fight for them and we fight for us. But if people can not go on living properly, what on earth are we actually fighting for? I have asked these questions a thousand times before but never got an answer. So I stand before you now, under the influence of faith, carrying the disease of hope, and I ask you to respond!"

The energy in the church was unbound, yet the response was silent. My feelings denied, my thoughts unseen, yet I could feel my heart thumping, my lungs aching and my hands shaking. A gust of wind came running through the doors, it danced around me, with me, then settled on the ground between the pews. I let the air fall still. Silence was all that was left. Looking around, nothing had changed. How much of this was just in my head? I felt a fool, I hadn't expected much but I had exhausted my abilities to believe in anything at all.

Retracing my steps, I hurried back, the sky brightening above me. Perhaps the pond held answers. After a short walk back, I reached it.

There, in the middle of the trees, an expansive open area full of water. Moving forward, I watched as the golden sunlight cascaded through a thin layer of mist and onto the water. I found myself irresistibly drawn towards the pond, its tranquil allure captivating my senses. Each step I took brought me closer to its edge, and with each passing moment, the world around me seemed to fade into insignificance.

Leaning over, as I gazed upon my blurred reflection in the mirror-like water, a disquieting sensation began to gnaw at the depths of my being. Something was awry. As I focused closer, passing a hand through the rippling surface, I noticed a peculiarity. My reflection, distorted and warped, failed to mirror my visage faithfully. Perplexed, I peered deeper into this looking glass, desperately seeking answers that eluded me. The visage that stared back at me was not my own. It was a distorted reflection, its face covered in blood, its arms burned and twisted. A haunting echo of my existence, bearing an uncanny resemblance that sent a chill coursing through my veins.

My heart momentarily ceased its rhythmic dance within my chest. Panic surged through my every fibre, a tempestuous storm threatening to consume me whole. I frantically searched for an escape, my mind racing to comprehend the inexplicable, to find solace in the familiarity that had been so cruelly shattered.

I ran. My feet pounding against the earth, desperate to distance myself from the peril that lurked within the depths of that cursed pond. Past the end of the path and into the forest, where the brambles and tree roots did not like me at all and did their best to make me fall. But my desperate flight was abruptly halted, for before me rose an imposing wall, its presence growing with each glance. It loomed above me, an insurmountable barrier that seemed to taunt my futile attempts at escape.

The wall engulfed me, the more I looked, the more it seemed to grow, closing in on me with an oppressive weight. Panic coursed through my veins, threatening to overwhelm my senses, as I grappled with the terrifying realization that there was no way out.

My moment of panic was abruptly interrupted by a voice.

"Running away will do you no good, especially if it's in the wrong direction."

I glanced back, only to be met with an older man. His words hung in the air, an invitation to respond. Slowly, as I turned to face him fully, I was met with a crooked grin that almost challenged the boundaries of his face. A smile that resonated deeply within me, almost as if we had met before.

CHAPTER 3

Turning to face him, I was struck by the many lines that ran across his face, suggesting an extraordinary amount of experience. Mr Buttons was his name, an older gentleman, who settled politely under a long overcoat, his peppercorn beard tickling the top of his scarf.

I studied the creature, watching as he pivoted on his cane and walked away. He had a limp and appeared to swing his left leg out from under his torso to move forward.

"Is this hell?" I blurted to him.

The man stopped. "Why do you ask?" he said, turning toward me.

"I'm wondering if I'll be judged." I admitted.

A gentle smile played upon his lips. "Life is not a talent show. There is no audience to perform for, no need for approval or tests, no admiration or power to attain. There is no one to convince. There never has been."

His words washed over me, a sense of hope developing. If anyone had answers, it would be him.

"Will you take me back?" I asked, my voice steady.

He nodded, a knowing smile playing upon his lips, and gestured for me to follow.

Together, we ventured forward, the guide taking short strides as I struggled to match his pace. As we moved on through the greenery, I spotted some old grandfather clocks nestled within the thick undergrowth.

I turned to my guide. "What's with the clocks?"

He did not react, nor did he answer.

"You don't talk very much, do you?"

The man stopped and turned to face me. "The more one talks, the less the words mean."

I chuckled, "Well, I'm going to keep asking questions until I get answers."

He remained serious, the same expression etched across his face, "When you find an opportunity, you might as well knock. You never know what doors will open."

His dead-end replies felt rather mocking, although I didn't have another alternative. We continued walking on our way to nowhere, onto the dirt path, past the map, off the beaten track, over a river and through some overgrowth.

"We are here."

"Here?" I replied. "How will I know which way to go from here?"

Mr Buttons paused and cast a glance in my direction. "Where is your destination?"

"Well, I don't know where I'm going."

"Then surely any direction is the right direction."

I didn't know how to respond. The man's responses puzzled me. He didn't provide the answers to my questions, but he gave me hope I would find the answers to mine.

"Can you at least tell me where we are?" I asked.

"I don't know. I'm only the gardener." he replied.

By this time, the storm had caught up with us and it started to rain once again.

"Well, who do you work for? What is the name of this garden?"

I never got a reply as, without warning, the guide seemed to vanish. Within a second of turning my back to him, he disappeared. Ever since I found myself here, I knew something was wrong, but his sudden disappearance made me even more certain something was amiss.

I decided to head to higher ground, hoping I'd be able to see where I was. But almost as soon as I started walking, I spotted a pointed spire peering from behind a fringe of trees. I walked cautiously towards it, my footsteps my only company. Soon enough, I had reached the entrance to some kind of house. Beyond them, a huge drive lay before me with tall dark trees on either side. I stood staring at the brown cast iron gates in the distance and the beautiful drive that lay beyond. As I approached, they began to open, an invitation to enter.

I began my ascent. It was a long and lonely walk, with only the cello-sounding creaks of the trees to keep me company. As the drive curved, the house slowly came into view. It was a huge structure, gothic-like, made of red terracotta clay brick, with stone arches and a fantastic amount of ornamental detail.

I moved closer, craning my neck back to take in the massive structure. Atop the house sat an imposing clock tower that immediately seized my attention. The clock's hands were frozen in place, unmoving. I stared, mesmerized, losing all sense of time and place. How long had I been gazing up hypnotically when the clock suddenly chimed, the deafening sound jolting me violently back to reality? I jumped, heart racing. I had been certain the clock was frozen. Pulse pounding, I scanned the surrounding area. My breath caught in my throat as I noticed a wheelbarrow towards the bottom of the garden. The grounds that surrounded the house teemed with love. Someone was living here.

I lingered outside, pacing up and down. Not that it mattered, but upon finding I couldn't see inside the house, I became terribly anxious. What lay beyond those walls?

As the rain fell harder, I found myself sheltering near the entrance. The door to the house was made of thick wood with lovely symmetrical carvings running across it. A beautiful marble green doorbell hung in the middle. I reached my hand, "Ting-a-ling!"

Silence.

I rang again and stepped back out into the rain. Looking up at the overhead window, I saw the curtains move, then heard movement on the stairs. I wanted to run again, but as my guide showed me before, running away is never the answer. The door opened slowly, and a boy's head appeared. He looked at me, his eyes penetrating my gaze.

"Yes?" he said.

I began to explain my situation to him. The boy, upon noticing my nervousness, smiled and moved out from behind the door. He stood and listened, appearing to take a personal interest in my suffering. As he did so, all of my apprehensions began to melt away, until I was left with nothing more than the feeling that I had met an old friend.

"You'd better come on in." he said.

A grand entrance hall met me as I wandered inside. Its walls adorned with carved oak, a gallery of photos stretching along either side and although I didn't recognise any of them, their familiarity made me feel as if I was looking back at memories from a previous life.

I quickly made my way past them, my feet gliding over the marble floor. Another double door was tucked away at the end. My sense of unease grew as we approached. The moment the second lot of doors swung open, I was immediately struck by a polite drone of classic music and a lingering smell of earthy incense.

Stepping inside, my eyes were drawn to a large oak fireplace, above which, sat a huge, magnificent floor-to-ceiling stained glass window which cast a kaleidoscope of colours that danced upon the plush furniture. A polished piano sat nearby, topped with various playful items from all corners of the world.

As I allowed my gaze to wander further, I discovered an alluring set of stairs nestled in the corner of the room. My eyes followed them up, and I was met again with the boy, leaning over a second-floor balcony.

"Where are your parents?" I asked.

"It's just me." he said.

"Well, when will your parents be back?"

"They won't. I live here alone. I look after myself, the house and the garden" he said, walking down the stairs.

"I'm sorry, but it's just- you look very small and very young."

"Judge me by my size do you?"

I didn't reply. I just stood watching him walk towards me. The house was filled with music, art plush furniture. How could such a person live here alone? That was if he was a person at all.

Moving towards the edge of the room I noticed how many artefacts, sculptures and paintings he had scattered about. A huge variety, appearing to come from all corners of the world. I soon found myself studying one of them, a statue of a snake.

I held it in my hand, moving my fingers across its metal skin. I had always had an interest in snakes. The way they shed their skin, changed and adapted to environments and the way people looked at them. It always fascinated me.

"What do you think?" the boy asked.

"An interesting animal, a symbol of rebirth to some, a symbol of fear to others." I replied.

"Oh yes," he said "you know, it's quite remarkable, to see how different people have different thoughts when they look at the same thing."

"Your house is quite beautiful. The art is simply perfect." I replied.

"Art isn't beautiful because it's perfect, it's beautiful because it makes us feel something."

He gestured for me to follow. We both walked into a rather splendid-looking kitchen. The kitchen was largely brown, in fact, most of the house was drowned floor to ceiling in wood, but my goodness was it full of life, full of art, full of detail. It was never boring. Not even for a second.

"Fancy a drink?" the boy said, now standing behind the kitchen island.

"Please, but aren't you too young to be drinking?"

"I'm offering tea. I do have stronger drinks, but they're over there in that cabinet."

I was already moving towards the cabinet, when I had to remind myself of my situation. Instead, I looked at the lights above the table, the fittings shaped like leaves. A stark contrast of beauty compared to the noise of the rain that piddled down against the windows. Who owns this kind of stuff? Certainly not a child. I watched as he made the tea, his mannerisms, his movements, they reminded me of someone.

In the corner of the room, I spotted a man in the mirror. "Aren't mirrors amazing?" I said to him.

The boy paused and looked up at my reflection "Who's he?"

"Nobody important." I replied.

The boy stared at me a little longer. "Your perception towards things tells a lot about your mindset y'know."

Taking a seat at the table, I felt the gentle touch of the blue velvet tablecloth against my palms. Next to me, a spacious bay window framed a view of the grounds. The young boy placed two cups of tea on the table and sat down beside me.

"You seem to know a lot about things. Tell me, who are you?" I asked.

"I'm just the gardener, really."

The same answer as Mr Buttons, was this perhaps the same person? All felt very odd.

"For a gardener, you don't seem very upset with the weather."

"Why would I be upset with the weather?" he said, looking puzzled.

"It's horrible," I said. "all this wind and rain."

"How I react to the rain won't change the fact that it's raining. I might as well be happy." he replied.

He was right, so much wisdom from someone so young. We sat and watched the cloud scatter, idle small talk hovering between us. Soon, the evening sun emerged from the rain, bathing the kitchen in warm purple hues.

"I can tell you are lost," said the boy "but where do you want to go?"

"I don't know." I replied.

"Well then, what do you need?"

These sorts of questions kept coming. For some odd reason I felt alone in not being able to answer. I wondered what this young boy thought of my dead-end replies. I was supposed to be setting some kind of positive example but if I couldn't even follow my own advice, what use was I to anyone? Despite this, I was surprised to find that the boy listened to me for over an hour, his attention set as though nothing else existed outside of our exchange.

"I'm sorry." I said. "I don't know what I'm doing, why I'm here. It's all so useless."

"It's okay to be lost." he said.

"I'm a failure." I replied.

The boy got up and walked over to the window "Sometimes we have to lose ourselves to find ourselves. It's all about perspective." he said picking up an old 8mm film camera that was sat on the windowsill. "Cameras have a special kind of magic. You can reframe the familiar and make the everyday seem extraordinary. That's why I adore them." he continued. "I want to show you something. Please, come and look through this."

I went over and looked through the eyepiece. I could see the window and the garden, in the distance I noticed a flower. The flower was hunched over from the weight of the water that stood on it's back.

"Do you see anything?"

"Yes, the garden." I replied.

I heard a click and the image shifted as he rotated to a new lens. A close-up this time. A single raindrop on the window, the garden and the sky reflecting through it from behind.

"Often, we don't get to choose what's in front of the camera. But we do get to choose how we view it, and sometimes, seeing things through a new lens can make all the difference."

I adjusted the lens so the image was in focus.

"You have the power to choose what you focus on." he continued. "It's about perspective. It works for a lot of things. Art can help remind us that we each view the world differently."

"I think you're right." I replied, still looking through the camera.

"I'm just going to start the fire," said the boy, "when you're done, feel free to help yourself to a drink over there." He nodded toward the cabinet and dashed for the door, stopping before it. "Just remember," he said, "it matters not what you look at, but what you see." and out he went, leaving me alone.

I immediately put the camera back and moved over to the cabinet, my addiction calling. I filled my glass and brought it to my lips.

The amber liquid coursed through my body, momentarily silencing the demons that haunted the caves deep within my mind. Before I could regret my decision, I swiftly moved back into the living room where the boy was sat quietly, prodding the hot embers with a firestick. Moving over to him I looked up at the window. The sky had now turned black, and the wind continued to howl.

Another prod from the firestick and the flames burst to life, it's heat licking at the base of my damp trousers. I still needed answers, so I went back to the art pieces at the side of the room. Strange how they looked different when under the influence. Moving across to the corner, I came across a bookshelf. My eyes flicked across it, coming to a stop at the sight of a bible.

The rage that resided inside me soon leapt onto its pages. Still there were no answers. I picked it up and held it in my hands, flicking through it as anger moved between my lips.

"I can think of no greater crime against the human race. To reduce the complexity of the universe, the depth and wonders of existence. To look at our intricate workings and assume we lack all innate sense of right and wrong. To claim that we must follow a set of rules and commands set out by an external authority in order to function. Oh, how dare he. We taught ourselves how to survive. We learned how to hunt, grow, harvest and cook. How to walk, talk and build. We made roads, bridges, rivers and dams. Created art, science and philosophy. We found ways to harness energy, to cure illnesses and to stop great forces of evil. We learned how to mine minerals from the earth and use them to improve our lives. With cars, cameras and computers, we learned how to travel across continents, to soar through the skies and to put man on the moon. Shakespeare, Galileo, Einstein, Picasso. Do they mean nothing? Why is it so frowned upon to credit our teachers, our mothers and our fathers? The people who nurtured us, who formed us. Humanity did those things, our ancestors. It's one thing to challenge science, but to claim our struggles, our innovations and our creations. There is nothing I find more insulting."

After my frustration left my mouth, I realised I had overstepped a line. "Sorry— I'm sorry." I gasped, "when I'm drunk, I often tell the truth."

The boy sat, saying nothing, looking at me from across the room. "Your words don't bother me, not at all. In fact, I don't think it matters what you believe in, as long as you believe in yourself. For we are not just creations, we are creators, and together we equal the whole. In that way perhaps we are all God. I admire your honesty. It takes great bravery to speak out about how you truly feel."

"It's not brave." I replied, putting the book back. " So often my sober thoughts become my drunken words. I should never question such things—"

"It's always good to question things." the boy interrupted. " One must be ready to question, able to believe and open to change. For without doubt we are easily deceived, without belief we learn nothing new and without change we cannot move forward."

"I haven't learned anything. I'm an alcoholic. I should know better." I cried.

"But you know better now. You're not in the past, you're in the present."

He didn't understand, and I hoped he never would. My drinking wasn't just part of the past, it was a part of me.

"The past shouldn't be a place to live in, it should be a place to learn from." he continued, "we shouldn't judge others based on what they were last seen being."

I walked over to the window, still sipping away at the whiskey. The boy moved beside me, watching me. "I'm sorry to ask this but, why drink when you know it will kill you?"

"I drink because I'm already being killed by something else. The dark doesn't hurt me, it's the things that live within it."

"That darkness, perhaps it's needed?" he replied, "the night teaches us that there's always beauty in darkness. Without the darkness, the stars wouldn't get a chance to shine."

I chuckled, looking down at the cup of whiskey as it swirled between my fingers. I knew he was trying to help but I was far past that point. I couldn't be angry, I would've done the same if I were his age.

"I see myself in you." I said to him.

"We've each got a part of each other." replied the boy.

We stood there for a moment, as I continued sipping away.

"Is this what being an adult is?" the boy continued, "finding ways to cope with the inevitable, paying taxes and then dying? I can't understand it, where's the fun?"

"Being an adult," I chuckled, "well, you're halfway there. I suppose being an adult is fighting to find you that you couldn't be when you were a child. It's learning that you don't have to be the 'you' others said you had to be when you were younger. It's learning to trim off the parts that you don't want and add the parts you always wanted but perhaps weren't allowed. It's also finding the unknown, undeveloped parts of you that you had to hide as a child and bringing them to the surface, to nourish or to learn to deal with. Sometimes those parts are hard to accept, but being an adult is a long process. Sometimes it takes a lifetime to find out who we really are. Yes, there are taxes and work. But that isn't what makes you an adult. Being an adult is realising that you make the rules, good or bad, for yourself now. Being an adult is being responsible for you, because only you get to decide who you are and what is best for you. It's difficult and it's not something you ever stop doing. Working on you is hard, but you have to fight for it."

"Are you going to fight?" said the boy.

I just looked at the stars.

"If you fight back, you'll have a chance, but not a guarantee. If you don't fight back, you'll have a guarantee and not a chance." he continued.

"I'll try." I said, handing back my glass.

He pointed at the stars and looked up at me. "The stars would be so proud to know their atoms came together to create someone like you."

Shortly after, the boy kindly asked if I would stay the night. Up over the balcony, round to the other side and into the guest room, where I spent the next hour watching the moonlight filter through the gap in the curtains. The hour after was spent staring at the sky. The darkness. The nothing. Trying to persuade myself that there was more. I had done everything right, I had searched for answers, knocked on doors, yet no one could cure my suffering and I remained a burden to all. Peering out the door, I found all was quiet except the howl of the wind and the pitter of rain. Without so much as a thought, I found myself slipping across the balcony, down the stairs, and into the kitchen to have another drink. Picking up my glass from the table, and over to the cabinet to quietly get the bottle. The lovely sound as it filled the glass.

There I was, sitting at the table, looking at the half-empty glass when the storm erupted. A bolt of lightning flashed outside, reflecting through the window in such a way that it made me remember. In a second, I was taken back to the pub, the road and the accident. I remembered everything. It was horrifying to remember, it was even more horrifying to understand. Jumping up from my seat, my eyes scanned across the room to a clock on the back wall. I watched as the second hand tilted backwards. I was right. I moved towards it, staring at the dials. Without any warning, there was a loud crack and the glass shattered, followed by the sound of thunder.

I stood, waiting for my mind to flounder across the no man's land between knowing the facts and knowing the feelings. I was on the cusp of death, the clocks around me ticking down to my final moment. But it all seemed so real, this. I was trapped and wasn't entirely certain where. All I knew is that I'd be better off dead. Instinctively, I found myself reaching for an old shopping list and writing out my emotions on the other side. Asking for forgiveness for something I hadn't done yet.

Dear,

I wish I didn't have to write these words, but I have held on to hope for far too long. I did everything I could. I studied hard, worked hard. I helped others and others tried to help me. But I could not help myself. This life is not for me. It is my time to go.

You won't understand my motives, and I hope you never do. But please know that this is the most painless way out for me. I've been suffering for years, my thoughts and feelings hurting more than blades ever could.

I could say so much more, but I won't. My secrets belong to me, and I keep them secrets so they don't hurt anyone else.

The only thing that matters is I won't be in pain anymore. I won't feel guilty about being in other peoples way, being a liability or a burden.

Please don't remember me as the man who failed to kill himself several times before succeeding. Remember me as the man who died several times and survived.

I am so grateful for your kindness, your words of wisdom and your hospitality. You're going to grow up to be an amazing person, believe me.

Goodbye.

I folded the note under the glass on the table and then I slipped out the side door.

CHAPTER 4

Descending the front lawn, the trees swallowing me whole. I sprinted faster, running until breathlessness forced me to stop. Gazing upward, I noticed a gap in the sky where the stars had vanished— a void, formed by the towering trunk of a tree, its dark mass blotting out the stars above.

I panicked, running deeper, until my feet met a gravel path that took me around to a pond. Carefully, I navigated its stepping stones, following the gravel up and round. The drive was beside me, but I couldn't find a way through. I pushed towards it, brambles tearing my skin as I moved through the bushes, out onto the drive and through the gates.

My arms were covered in blood, but it didn't matter. In the midst of depression all I thought about was getting out. Nothing else mattered. I would've killed myself sooner if I had the chance, but I didn't want a stranger to bear the result of my suffering.

Suicide had always been an odd subject for me. After my fathers death, the thought of such an act seemed not only selfish but insulting. How could one leave their own family to wallow in the question of "Why?" There are not enough words for me to describe the weight of sorrow that falls upon one after death, suicide or otherwise. To suffocate in one's grief is one thing, but to be the cause is another. It wasn't until I found myself standing where so many people had stood before me that I finally understood the reasons why.

Wind gust through the gates behind me, picking me up and carrying me down the hill back towards the river. Trailing off from the path, I found myself on the mossy river bank. Unbeknown to me, my solution lay only a few hundred yards or so upstream. I followed the water until I stumbled upon a large weathered stone bridge. I ran up the bank and up onto it, where I collapsed at its crest. Resting against it, out of breath, I realised that I had begun to sober up. One of the great things about being sober is you get your feelings back. One of the bad things about being sober is that you also, get your feelings back.

I sat, the rough stone abrading against my palms as I slid closer to the edge, my feet dangling over the river's glassy surface. If I were human, I would've hit the water by now, but I was not human. I was flesh, blood, meat and bone. I had left the thunder behind me, and the rain settled to no more than a wet breeze. Looking up, I saw the stars above glimmering. Oh, how I wished I could reach out my hand and pluck one from its path.

"This is it. This is it." I said.

The stars were silent. Once again, I was alone. Positioning myself above, not daring to look down into the water. For what monstrous visions would surface this time? I inhaled deeply, the air now filled with the urge to jump.

I was halfway off the bridge when I finally got the courage to look down into the murky depths. I was surprised to find that no reflection could be seen from within. The water echoed, and a soft splash from under the bridge caught me by surprise. Looking down, I saw the rhythmic dip of oars cutting through water. A small wooden boat followed, piloted by the same young boy whom I met earlier.

He looked up at me. "Before you jump, as I think you might, please listen to what I have to say!"

He positioned the boat beneath me, where he began his speech. "Think of yourself when you were young, the places you saw, the songs you sung. That same little boy who played with cars, he never thought you'd get this far. He thought of who you are, who you might become, the things he'd accomplish, the joy and the fun. Dreams and hopes lit up his mind, a wonderful future he hoped to find. I'm sorry, this makes you sad I can see, not being the man you once hoped to be. My point is, you still have time to change. That little boy would hope this isn't how it ends. And what about the old man, all wrinkled and grey, who walks along the beach showing his kids how to play? You told me there's so much more you want to do, but don't you realise you would be killing him too?"

"I cannot say that older man is me, for I still don't know who I am yet." I replied.

"If you don't know who you are yet, why would you end your life? Why would you end your life when you don't know whose life you're ending?"

"I know who I am, I know who I want to be. Dead."

"But why?" the boy asked.

"I'm better off dead." I replied. "I wouldn't be a liability to others. The only thing stopping me is the thought of my death being another burden. I've thought about it for years. I wonder, if I died today. Who would attend my funeral—"

"Not me."

"Why?"

"I'd be at home, trying to work out where I went so wrong."

Sitting on the edge of the bridge, for the first time I found myself questioning my decision. The boy spoke of life as if hope was real, as if life was special. I began to wonder, what if he's right?

The boy looked up at me from the boat. "Jonathan, I can't understand your pain, but I see how you carry it. I see how it crushes you and how you choose to keep going despite it. I think I know why you hesitated to jump. You've suffered a long time, yet you continue to stay, not because it's easy but because you don't want to hurt the people around you. Every day of your life so far, despite the pain, you have chosen to stay. People rarely talk about this side of suicide, but every time you make that decision not to end things, you're making a sacrifice that most people can't even begin to understand. You're not a coward, you are not taking the 'easy way out.' You're fighting a battle every single day, and you're doing it out of love. I don't think you realise just how brave that is. Not only is it an act of incredible selflessness, but it is something quite extraordinary."

I was too stunned to reply.

"And if you ever find yourself without someone to live for, live for yourself." he continued. " Be here now, but do things that make younger you happy and older you proud. There is still time. This is your starting point, not the end. There are people out there waiting to meet you, waiting to love you. If you don't believe me, why not simply stay to find your new favourite movie, to find your new favourite food? Or just to prove people wrong. The truth is, there is so much to do here. There are so many books you have left to read. There are so many instruments to play, songs to hear, foods to try, places to go. So why not add some more lines to your smile? Let the silver hairs sprout from your cranium. Don't you want to become the person you've always meant to be? Don't you want to get clean? There is no right way to recover, but there is a wrong way, that is if you don't try to recover at all."

He rowed the boat out even further in front of me and stood up.

"Jonathan, look." he said pointing to the trees beside the river bank. "Before those trees grew, they took the time find their roots. They took nourishment from the soil and found their place in the earth. The roots are the most important part of the tree, yet they are unseen and unfelt. You are learning and growing. You just don't see it.

Some of these trees are the same age as you, growing alongside you. You have never been alone."

I began to cry. After I promised to give tomorrow a chance, he talked me down from the bridge and onto a path that ran beside the river.

"The sun will rise soon and it'll be the first day of the rest of your life. The start of a new chapter." he said.

"I don't think I'm ready to start a new chapter." I replied.

"Give tomorrow a chance. I know moving forward can be frightening, but staying in the same place seems even more horrific, doesn't it? "

We ventured forward down the river, him in the boat, me walking beside him on the land.

"How old are you?" I asked.

"9."

"How long have you been 9?"

"A while." he chuckled.

Strange how someone could be so knowledgeable. He had made the dream feel real. I didn't want it to feel real.

"I'm curious, have you any idea what you want to do with your life? Who do you want to be?" the boy asked.

"A writer, but I don't think I'm very good."

"Nonsense. Your writing is special. I think you have something beautiful to add to the world. I truly mean that."

I smiled at him. "And who do you want to be?" I asked the boy.

"Like you."

"Why?"

"You're so brave. Imagine if we all had the bravery to express how we truly feel? So many romanticise dying for someone, but living for someone, especially when every day feels like torture, that's real courage. I wish more people could understand it, because every time you decide to keep going, you're showing a kind of strength that most people will never know. I see that in you, and it makes you a hero in my eyes. The fact that you're still here, despite everything, speaks to a kind of bravery and sacrifice that deserves to be recognised."

Grinning like a fool, I wiped the tears from my face. As soon as I did so, I heard screams. The river had abruptly transformed before my eyes.

I heard one splash, then two, I turned around only to see the boys hands reaching through the water. The tranquil waters had boiled into violent rapids, frothing and churning with primordial fury. The boy's small boat was capsized and hurtled downstream. His frightened cry pierced my heart.

"Follow the current, don't fight it!" I yelled, desperate to save him from the jagged rocks that awaited. As I glimpsed his face more clearly in the chaos, recognition shuddered through me. Round cheeks, eyes shining with optimism and promise — it was a younger version of me, untarnished by life's blows.

My stomach dropped as his boat abruptly capsized, plunging him into the raging torrents. "No!" I screamed, watching helplessly as the rapids pummelled his small body. He surfaced, gasping, only to be sucked back down into the maelstrom. I jumped in after him.

CHAPTER 5

As we sank into the abyss, our fingertips touched for a brief moment before the current took him away. I clawed toward him, searching frantically through the rolling chaos until my vision began to turn black.

With my hands stretching to the sky, I broke the surface, flailing violently to keep afloat, the river laughing at me as it gurgled. I managed a single gasp of air before the current sucked me under, spinning my body in a rag-doll fashion. I closed my eyes tightly as I anticipated the inevitable smash against the jagged rocks along the riverbank. That violent moment never arrived, but I was still in survival mode.

After being tossed around by the currents, it was a relief to feel the river propel me into open water. I knew I had gotten away safely from the shore, but I was finding myself wanting to swim no more. The young boy had helped sowed the seeds of belief, belief in change. But now I had lost him, I had solidified my belief that I was vulnerable to illusions and lies.

Rendering myself useless, I surrendered to the water. My feet travelling towards the darkness, sinking down further as if an invisible force was pulling on them. When all fell silent, my body was picked up and carried politely across what felt like the ocean floor, being brushed against plants, rocks and soft sand. I did not intervene, for my mind still wandered, only coming back when I felt my knees settle in the sediment at the bottom.

Kneeling there, on that cold floor, I realised that this was rock bottom. The lowest I had ever been. I was surrounded by dark ocean, unexplored and vacant. My eyes saw darkness and all I could see was failure. But finally, I was at peace, left alone with only myself for company.

I tried to stay silent, but the murky depths threatened not only to drown the man but the frightened boy who still lingered within. Even there, at the bottom of that ocean bed, I wondered if it was possible to drown in something else other than my thoughts.

My world was ending so quietly. Despite wanting this for so long, I could never have imagined actually going through with it. I'd always hoped my life would go out with a bang, perhaps some natural disaster, an atomic war, or even a robbery gone wrong. One final chance to be part of the pack, to fit in, to die a hero or die with dignity.

My primal fears had already begun to take over, the ones that gripped me as a child. The fear of monsters lurking under the bed, the fear of heights, the fear of dark. It was then that I realised that all it ever was, was the fear of the unknown.

My lungs began to spasm, bits of me spilling out onto the ocean floor. My body was screaming for me to take a breath. I was scared. I hated that feeling, but at least I felt it. This was the first time my death occurred to me as a reality, and as strange as it seems, as I accepted my fate, a moment of peace was born from my surrender.

Opening my eyes for the final time, I saw a miracle. The sun had started to rise and the water began to calm. When the water calmed, clarity came. There was something so beautiful about being on the edge of life and death. Watching the sun reflect on the water as the dark spots started to fill my eyes. Both horrifying and beautiful. Standing side by side the two, playing, flirting, shaking hands. It was almost exhilarating.

Being on the bottom of it all, I could see the potential above me. I had the freedom to swim in any direction, to go wherever I pleased. The sea was endless. It was just me and possibility in every direction. The dots had almost filled half my vision when I changed my mind. Everything was beautiful when I knew it was the last time I was going to see it. So it was then that I pushed off from the ocean bed. The ground beneath me felt wonderfully solid, and it was strangely comforting to know I could fall no further. That was the day the endless sea of darkness became known to me as the endless sea of opportunity.

With a gasp I broke the surface, heaving violently. I lay back exhausted, feeling the blanket of water wrap around me. I stretched out my limbs and relaxed my body, my mind wandering above me while I lay still. The sea kept my body afloat, but it had claimed the spirit of my soul. Well, not claimed in its entirety. Rather, borrowed, kidnapped and forced to walk through untouched areas of my mind. Places where illusions were born, answers turned to questions and even the happiest memories birthed their own guilt.

Throughout the night, the current continued to dance around my body, rocking me back and forth like a mother rocking her crying baby. Eventually, placing me down on a cot of warm sand, a kiss of salt planted firmly between my lips.

I awoke to sunlight piercing through my eyelids. I squinted against dazzling sunlight to see palm trees swaying above me, and beyond them, the endless expanse of a sparkling blue ocean.

I looked around. Rocks on the shore shone in the light. The waves murmured to the sand. But the beach went on endlessly with not a soul in sight. I stumbled to my feet, strolling along, my sodden clothes chafing with each weary step. Footsteps disappearing almost as soon as they were made.

As I walked, a lump rose in my throat. Up ahead in the distance, a small sandcastle came into view. I carried myself towards it, whispering my hopes and secrets to the sand. As I got closer, I saw that the base had been worn down by the tide. Someone had left a small handwritten sign jutting from the tallest turret. It read:

"We had so much fun on that hot summer day. I'm still real in your memory, but now I'm washed away."

I sank to my knees before it, memories of a long-ago summer day flooding back. My young self had built this very castle, laughing joyfully as the sun baked his bronzed shoulders. The words pierced my heart. That innocent child full of hopes and dreams, what would he think of the man I had become? I had promised him so much.

Something strange about the way things stayed the same. My insides had shifted, the larger cog had twisted and the tension was high. I was in a different place— physically that is. Mentally, I hadn't moved an inch.

The day slipped on as I casually handed all of my time away to grief. I couldn't help it, grief will do that. It'll warp your perspective, change the things in which your reality revolves around, and if it's kind enough it will erase your capacity to feel at all. When the pain gets so bad the mind can not grasp onto it with any sort of meaningful level of consciousness, it recoils back into itself unable to take it. Sometimes, when the pain is so clear and real in its purity and strength, the only thing we can do to protect ourselves is make it abstract.

Seated on the beach. I picked up a handful of sand and let it slip through my fingers, the cool sea breeze carrying it over the water. I glanced up at the sky, now painted with a hundred different shades of red. The end of another wasted day.

"I'm so sorry," I choked out.

The surf had risen steadily, waves licking at the sandcastles base. Soon, the incoming tide would wash it away for good. My past, dissolving before my eyes. I felt guilty when I spent time with grief and I felt guilty when I didn't. There was nothing I could do to change the past, but how dare the world keep moving on without me. It was a terribly cruel thing. I was still processing yesterday, when tomorrow had already begun.

I sat and watched as the last turret slumped into the sea. Exhaustion pressed upon my heart. I fell backwards in the sand, arms curled around my heaving chest. Anguish tore through me as the truth sank in, I had failed. The river had claimed the boy and with him, all hope of reclaiming my lost innocence. Hot tears spilled down my cheeks, lost amidst the endless sea.

I lay alone on the desolate beach, head in hands, shards of my broken spirit piercing my heart. As the embers of dusk engulfed the shore, a familiar voice spoke.

CHAPTER 6

I was sitting on the sand, my thoughts buried deep within it, when the voice spoke.

"Isn't it beautiful?" it said.

A moment of silence settled the air.

"Sometimes I come down here just to feel the waves beneath my feet. To admire this beautiful game we call life." it continued.

Turning towards it, I found Mr Buttons. His eyes were already looking directly at me, filled with great concern.

"Life may be a beautiful game, but I wish I never played it." I replied.

Mr Buttons moved beside me.

"Jonathan." he said, quite sternly. "You know you only have to do this once."

"Do what?" I replied.

"Live." he cried.

A moment passed in silence.

"Thank god, I hate this shit."

Mr Buttons chuckled. "You are very polite about your demons. I see you don't want to put the pain onto anyone else."

"Anyone else!" I snapped. " No one else understands! They never will! I don't even know why I'm here, or what I'm supposed to be doing. It all seems so pointless!"

"I'm sorry, you seem angry—"

"Of course I'm angry. Do you have any idea how many times someone should have helped me!?"

Mr Buttons was silent for a moment, the waves crashing beneath his feet. "Listen, I can't tell you I understand, because I don't. But I can tell you I care, because I do."

"Why?" I asked. "I'm just an alcoholic, that's all I am. I'd think myself lucky to be known as a loser."

" Jonathan, you're not a bad person for the ways you try to fight your inner evil."

Something about Mr Buttons composure eluded me. As my eyes fell up to his I could see that he did, in fact, care.

"I've often tried to drown my demons." I said finally.

"Tried?" he replied. "Did it work?"

"No, the assholes learned how to swim."

Mr Buttons smiled, I couldn't help but smile back.

"That's the first time I've seen you smile." he said, beaming.

"What is your name?" I enquired.

"Just call me Mr Buttons."

"Mr Buttons, you're an amazing person but please don't feel you need to waste your energy on me. I'm just a struggling alcoholic."

"Why does that matter?" he remarked. " I'm just a gardener."

"No. you're an angel. You have saved my life."

"And you made me laugh for the first time in a long while." he replied.

"Are you depressed too?" I asked.

"No, but it's difficult to find flowers that do stand up."

Mr Buttons stood up and offered me his hand, which I was afraid to take. I stood up beside him. We turned our backs to face the sea and walked into the night.

Our path wound and twisted, our two shadows mingling together amongst the trees.

"I'm sorry for shouting earlier." I said.

"Please, don't be. Guilt is often a waste of time."

"It's just, I feel so lost." I replied. "I worry. I don't know where I am... I want to know what my purpose is- I want to know- "

Mr Buttons stopped and turned to me. "Why does everything have to have meaning or purpose?"

"What is life without it?"

"It's anything you want it to be." he replied.

We moved forward, my legs driving me towards the sky. This continued for a while. We sailed across the hills and danced from cloud to cloud until eventually we reached a meadow of flowers. Past the hedge, over the turnstile and through the gate. Mr Buttons leading the way.

"Please" he gestured, taking off his coat and laying it on the ground.

I sat and looked around. We were surrounded by flowers but the sun had already parted between the hills, making it too dark to enjoy the view. The minutes ticked on by. Idle chatter fluttered in the air. We sat and waited, watching as darkness combed through the sky and settled deep within the trees.

I didn't know this at the time, but this was the start of one of the most powerful and beautiful conversations I had ever had the pleasure to be a part of.

"I'm sorry, but is this it? All that walking just to lie on a wet patch in a field?" I questioned.

"You missed watching the sunset, listening to the birds fall silent, seeing the stars dance in the night sky… enjoyment is often in the journey, not the destination."

"Well, it's a bit different when the destination is death, the final end." I replied. "What's the point? We're just here in this endless space of nothingness, living our lives, not even bothering to think about why we're even here. Being such tiny, insignificant things, and living in a universe that's too big to ever fully explore or see."

"You're right." he said. "Compared to the size of the universe we are small and insignificant, but you've got to keep it in perspective. We're lucky really, I mean think of the odds of you existing at all. The universe went through a billion acts of chance that led to you being conceived, millions of chemical reactions occurred just to make you, you. Think of all the potential people that could have been but didn't get the chance. Look around. The mere fact that the universe is so large and yet we are able to be here like we are is amazing. We are unlike any other planet or species in the universe. Don't look at it all and think we're insignificant. We're the equivalent of someone finding a diamond the size of a grain of sand on a beach the size of Mars. We are small, but we ARE significant"

"That may be true, but still, we're only here for 80 years or so."

"Oh, of course." he exclaimed. "Everyone knows you cannot control the length of your life, but you can control its width and its depth. We're not entitled to 80 years, in fact we're not entitled to anything at all. None of us know how much time we have left, that's why we should enjoy every moment."

"How can I enjoy every moment when it only took a moment for everything to change?"

"Life is full of good and bad moments, but none of them are ever unbearable." he replied.

Sitting there, in that long cold grass I felt that my guard had been completely abandoned and I had opened myself completely. I was beautifully vulnerable, open to the world, to new ideas, opinions and ways of thinking. Looking over at him, I wondered, how can one be so positive in the face of death.

"Are you worried?" I asked. "Are you not worried about what comes next?"

"No, I used to worry so much about what came next, that I often forgot that I was right in the middle of what I used to look forward to. Worrying about the inevitable won't prevent it from happening. That includes death. We all come from a long line of death."

"I'm still scared of it. " I exclaimed.

"We only fear death because it's the unknown. No matter your views on it, it's not going to change the fact that right now you're here, living. Be here now. Stop worrying about things that might turn out to be alright. I do not fear death, for I have been dead far longer than I have ever lived. It's not a crime to be dead. 99.9% of every species that has ever lived is dead. It's very fashionable these days."

"What do you think happens after we die?"

"After we die?" he repeated. "After we die, we decompose. We become food for plants. We are walking, talking, thinking plant food. If you want to be depressing, you could argue that this is our only real purpose in life. We are born. We use the earth to live. We die, we go back into the earth. Our bodies break down. The atoms disassemble and find new uses elsewhere."

"If we're buried in a coffin aren't our atoms contained there forever?" I asked

"Eventually the coffin will decay. Our body will be absorbed back into nature and broken down by bugs and bacteria.

"So we become dirt?" I said. " Stupid useless dirt."

"My dear boy, you would be surprised. The soil beneath our feet is absolutely brimming with life. We often spend too much time looking up to the sky that we fail to notice the life beneath our feet. I love making soil. Layering plants, food and waste in just the right amounts. Feeding, watering and turning it as needed. Holding it in my hand as I feel the heat from the trillions of unseen bacteria. Watching as it transforms it right before my eyes. Nurturing it so it can sustain life. Life! The same life that me and you possess. It's an entire universe in itself. When I eat food that has been grown with my compost I get the satisfaction that I have created a circle of life. I put some of that energy right back into the soil and then use it. It doesn't matter if we are plants, animals or people. Decomposition is just a part of the circle of life.

The mere fact that when we die, our bodies will be broken down by bacteria, insects, fungi, and will be used by plants and animals gives me so much more comfort than any afterlife ever could. We do live on, we help sustain new life. We go back to the earth. Back to the universe. Right where we came from."

"I don't relate to any of this." I proclaimed. "I'm from the city."

"Of course you do!" he gasped. " Life is all about perspective. What about the plants on your balcony?"

"But I only have a couple of flowers."

"Flowers. Every flower goes through stages of budding, opening, closing and wilting. Each of them has a preferred season and environment. They are unique. Like us. Each of us is unique. And like flowers, we each have a preferred season. So why do we expect ourselves to be in bloom all year round?"

"But flowers are beautiful even when closed."

"Nature does not strive for beauty. It lives, learns, adapts and changes over time. It only strives for functionality. Yet we find it so beautiful. Maybe we should spend more time doing these things. Living to the fullest. In doing so, we may become beautiful. We are in constant transformation, both spiritually and physically. Our bodies are our physical landscape and growth, even in the most rugged situations, is not destitute. Life is still all around us. All things are possible from the source."

Something inside me started to shift. But I still found myself wondering, how could one be so positive? Especially in the face of death.

"Do you believe in God?" I asked. " Is that how do you stay so positive?"

"No, I don't believe in God, but I can see why people do. Religion is great at providing comfort as it attempts to describe the universe we live in, why we die, and why certain things happen. But like everything in life, we can only see and judge through our own eyes. It's a part of why I believe in not just diversity, but inclusivity. We shouldn't judge how others react to it."

"Well then, how do you cope? How do you live?"

"I just try to find life in helping others where I can, by being a decent human being, by not taking too much, by giving back. We're all God. We all have the power to change the world, to make it a better place, no matter how small that change may be. Doing something is always better than doing nothing. My advice applies to my hobbies too, y'know I garden, I create, I listen to music, but most importantly, I listen to myself. I do the things I want to do. I spend time with myself."

He turned to look at me. "Often, we must find something to look forward to. It can be anything." he exclaimed. "Literature is always good. Stories are particularly powerful because they support the illusion that life has direction and purpose. Where God fails to show his hand, the writer shows his. When so much around us seems meaningless, stories give meaning. Stories don't judge, yet they teach us, nurture us and while life goes on, they do us the favour of ending."

He paused for a moment, looking up at the stars.

"Sometimes all you need is a reminder to take a second and look around." he continued. "A reminder to see how wonderful this all is and to put yourself into perspective against the universe. At the end of the day, we're just a bunch of evolved monkeys, sat round a campfire, orbiting the sun on a large rock. Nothing will matter when the sun decides to swallow us whole. Do I have a perfect life? Of course not.

There are times when I find it's all too much. Times when I hide away inside under the covers of darkness. But that's only temporary. It always will be. It may pass like a kidney stone, but it'll pass. It's a silly phrase but it's true. For now, we just have to learn to find enjoyment and reasoning in our life, then hold onto that until the end. The world revolves around love. Love one another, always. Be kind, for every single person you meet is living for the first time. We're all scared, believe me. None of us know what we're doing, we're making it up as we go. But we're lucky. We got a chance to live, we got the roll of the dice. Now we must take it and run with it. We're all in this together. All of us, hand in hand walking each other home."

He looked at the wrinkles on his palms and began to tear up. "Don't waste this Jonathan." he said, "Make the most of it. Celebrate every moment, every breath. Live your life as though you have everything you need. Be glad for every day you wake. Go outside, explore, chat for hours under the stars. Stay up late playing games, go out with your friends. Indulge, but don't try and cut your life short. Be silly, have fun, smile and laugh. Learn what you like, what you love and what makes you happy. This is such a valuable experience that we don't get twice. Do establish goals and things to strive for, but make sure you enjoy the journey. Wake up early and enjoy the misty grey before sunrise, stay up all night and feel that chill as the cold hour sets in and ultimately gives way to growing warmth, experience and learn what you love in life. Get out there. Fill yourself with joy and fulfilment. Make others smile, make others laugh, be happy. Above all else: Don't wait for your 'moment'. This is your moment. Enjoy life now. There are many causes people will commit their lives to, find something you love that you'll push yourself every day to keep living for. Could be joy, could be spite at the futility of it all, but keep living. Your meaning is out there. Make it. Find it. Grab it. Never let it go. Live for yourself, live for others. But live. Live."

That was the last of our conversation, but it was the start of something else. Of course, I was still full of doubt. But this was the shift from victim to fighter. Observer to participant. The boy told me the sun would rise again and now I believed him. I had finally chosen to act on my emotions, to ask questions and to seek answers.

Lying there, under the stars, I felt such possibility. Mr Buttons was my saviour. I had visions of us going for walks, fishing by the river, having conversations that helped me, such silly things, but for me, life-changing conversations. It never occurred to me that I was in one of those moments which I dreamed about.

I fell asleep at the edge of tomorrow, wondering which dreams would survive the night

CHAPTER 7

57

It was the day I fell in love with being alive. I found myself lying on the ground, staring at the sky shortly after sunrise. The beautiful sky. I lay sprawled out, taking deep breaths. The air charged with an energy I had long forgotten existed.

Guilt still pressed down on me, but I refused to wallow in it and decided to act on it. To retrace my steps, seeing if I could find the house and the boy, my younger self.

I rose slowly from the floor, brushing leaves from my clothes, joints stiff from a night on the hard ground. I looked around. It was if I was seeing the world for the first time. The world full of colour. Yellowing sunlight kissed every corner of the landscape, wonderful shades of green faded to blue and orange near the horizon. There I was, in the middle of it all. I finally felt at home, I was no longer seeing the world in black and white. It was beautiful. Clouds still shuffled across the sky, but I did not see them as full of rain. They had a purpose, a meaning. They added contrast to my otherwise plain sky.

As I moved on through the meadow, I gave myself the freedom to wander, to get lost. To be free. I wasn't chained to myself and my insecurities. I found myself looking at things I had never seen before. Little details. I noticed how the flowers nodded in the wind, the trees arched and the grass swayed. There is magic in those little moments. Maybe they were here before but I never paid attention. I saw all parts of the rose, not just the thorns. I found myself enjoying the simplicity of it all.

Moving down the end of the meadow and into a field of grass, I reached out my arms. There were so many different types of grass, soft, hard, long and short. I enjoyed noticing, feeling, running through them as the wind combed their tops. How much easier would our lives be if we could learn from these observations? To follow the wind of life and not always resist it, I thought.

Moving down through the trees, I soon came across the graveyard again. I approached from a different side, and looking over the fence I could see hundreds of other graves I hadn't noticed before. I was only passing by but made I decided to go and apologise to Mr Henderson.

I had my doubts about walking through that gate. It felt wrong to visit again so soon. Temperaments of anger still lingered in the air, but this was what remembering was. This was what it was to have been alive.

Mr Henderson's grave was largely the same, but before I started my apology, I noticed something tucked under a rock on the floor below. It was another note.

Jonathan,

Please don't be sad. I may have died, but I did not disappear. Death is not the end. It's simply a transformation, a form of change. Our bodies live on in nature, our souls live on in art.

When I was alive, my body was home to an ecosystem made up of millions of tiny creatures. They lived inside me, on my skin, and in my gut. After my death, those microbes worked tirelessly to break down my body, returning everything I borrowed back to nature and sending my molecules off in a billion new directions.

As Einstein once said, energy cannot be created or destroyed, it can only change from one form to another. He was right. The cells that made up my body now mingle and dance with the earth beneath your feet. I hope the bugs and worms have a wonderful feast. Birds will carry pieces of me into the sky, I will become part of the food chain, part of the cycle of life. Nature will carry me into the soil and water, and through the natural process of decomposition, they'll help make sure that everything I once was becomes part of the earth again.

Every atom of mine was once formed in a star. Every one of those atoms passed through millions of organisms on its way to becoming me, and they will continue to pass through the universe long after. I have simply returned home.

I am now a part of everything. I am water, I am life. I am the rain that falls, the trees that shelter, the compost that grows. So look around in all you see, you may even encounter a piece of me.

Mr Henderson.

As I stood there and thought about my own life, I began to grasp the meaning, scale and beauty of his words. Strange, how a letter from a man I hardly knew could teach me so much. But Mr Henderson was right, people do live on, but not only in nature and art, but in others too. We are the products of the people around us, and they are the products of us. Everything connected.

Moving gently across the graveyard, familiar words started to appear on the graves around me. Stones held memories of people, events and interactions. Passing by them, I started to remember, learn and appreciate the past. I began to see fragments of people in the way I walked, talked, even in the way I made my tea. Phrases that appeared under my breath became recognisable, taken from old friends long ago.

My feet took me to the edge of the graveyard, and started to advance beyond, my curiosity etching towards a clearing between the hedges. But the graves loomed over my shoulder, "Be still" they whispered "listen and never forget, you are the result of the love of thousands. Even our faces are mosaics of people who fell in love."

It was a fascinating thing, to recognise the contributions others had made in my life, even the small things shaped and moulded me. Even now, I still sign my name off with a smiley face because my favourite teacher used to do the same. When making tea I always put the sugar in first because that's how grandma liked it best. I only got into playing ping-pong because a boy I met on holiday taught me how to play. I still tie my scarf in a double knot because a kind stranger at the bus stop showed me how.

It didn't matter who they were, everyone I had ever interacted with had influenced me. From the shopkeeper down the street, neighbours I see twice a year, to close family who passed away. Some of whom I hadn't thought about for years, some I didn't even know the names of, and some I knew I would never see again. Brief moments of human exchange, footsteps in the garden, each with little marks made.

This was the art of noticing.

Advancing through the clearing, I found myself being swept up a hill towards a chimney that was peering through the canopy of trees. This was the way to the boys home I thought. No. Only a few steps later and my breath caught in the back of my throat. It was the home I had lived in as a child.

Cautiously, I moved closer. Strange how we pass through time, year after year, without so much as a thought. It's only when we notice how things have changed, that we realise how the years have flown. My heart pounded as I climbed the steps to the porch. This was an exact replica of the home I lived in as a child. Down to the marks on the door and the curtains in the window.

You might think that in twenty-odd years I'd forget, let the details and feelings sink far enough that I could not retrieve them with any certainty of truth. But you'd be wrong. Stepping through that door, I allowed myself to enter the world I knew as a child. As the door closed softly with an echoed thud, I found myself remembering everything.

In odd moments like that, you can feel your memory gathering its material, like an artist digging out old paints. The canvas is prepared, the tools are laid out, and soon old hands find themselves gliding across the canvas as effortlessly as they did yesterday.

Looking into the kitchen beside me, everything was as I remembered it. I lived in this house for years, it was here that I said my first words and took my first steps. Where I had my birthday parties and ate my cake. Out of the back window, I saw the garden where I learnt to climb trees, ride a bike, and where I finally figured out how to use a skipping rope.

I trailed my fingers across the kitchen counter where we shared so many moments together. There is a chance I may remember these memories too fondly. Nostalgia is strange like that, but time is something else. Time is a funny thing. You're young your whole life, until suddenly you're not. One day your grandparents are old, full of wisdom and love. The next they're tired, in pain and then they're gone. The pet you've grown up with, the cat or dog. The one that welcomes you home with such love. Growing beside you, shedding hairs, one day you find is no longer there. Your parents are young, invincible, and strong. Always there for you, until they too get sick and fade away. Leaving behind empty chairs and silent rooms where one once played. You wake up one day to find all the continuous, constant sources of love are no longer around. You wish somehow to go back in time, even just for a minute or two. To absorb those moments in a way you didn't before. Back when a trip to the shop meant your parents took care of it all. To sit with your grandparents as they cooked up a roast. To be carried out of the car after a long trip and tucked straight into bed. To feel the dog licking your face when you were sad. The simple joys of life, being able to jump out of bed without your back aching. Being able to hug your mum or dad whenever you want. Time is everything we have and the only thing we don't. It's no one's fault. When that's all we've ever known, how are we supposed to know it had to change?

"Hello? Anyone home?" I shouted, hoping for a response.

I moved on through to the living room, taking a moment to appreciate my old home and the things that lived within it. Upon noticing the back door open, I went through to the garden and garage. The place was empty, but my memories tried to fill in the gaps.

The garage, where my father used to spend most of his time. Everything was as it was. My dad's tools, laid out as if he were coming back. Everything as it was before, but missing the most important piece. I stared at it all, aching from the empty silence. It wasn't his death that hurt me, it was the things that proved he was alive.

It felt so wrong to move or touch his things. He was coming back, or so I thought. It's fascinating how grief suddenly makes the meaningless stuff so meaningful. Even the small things almost forced me to my knees, a teabag left in his cup, a piece of his hair on the workbench.

With hot tears streaming down my face, I started to think about it all. One day he picked me up, put me down and never lifted me up again. He did the same with his tools, his cup and his apron. Did he know it would be the last time? Did he ever think about it? I imagined that if I stood in the garage long enough, he would burst back through the door with a smile on his face, pick up his tools and continue hammering away, right from where he left off. Perhaps he would just call my name from the garden. Perhaps… My thoughts didn't reside further than that— I didn't let them. For sometimes, for our own self-preservation, we must deny ourselves to dream. I learned quickly that time doesn't stop when you need it to.

Standing in the living room, I halted abruptly. In the corner sat the liquor cabinet, crystal decanters and bottles glinting in the dim light. My heart stuttered. Suddenly, the cravings I had battled so long came crashing down around me.

"Just one drink." my addiction whispered. "One can't hurt now." My hands shook, clasping the cabinet doors. I held the bottle, imagining the burn of whiskey sliding down my throat.

From far away, I heard my mums voice pleading for me to wake up sober. I looked at the bottle. "No," I gasped, "I don't need it anymore." Defiantly, I smashed it on the floor.

A groan resounded through the house. I stumbled back in shock as the liquor cabinet began to burst into flames, dark smoke filling the air.

"Just take me with you," my addiction's sinister voice urged, "you know you can't make it without me." Before I realised what I was doing, I opened the doors and reached inside for a six-pack, the fire scorching my skin. With trembling hands, I cracked open one of the cans of beer.

Shame and self-loathing washed over me. What was I doing? I had come so far, and now I was throwing it all away, letting the darkness win. But instead of drinking from the can I had nearly succumbed to, I hurled its contents into the flames in defiance. The fire sizzled and died out.

Upon hearing noises above, I frantically raced upstairs, checking each room. All were empty, but the last one left a lump in my throat. It was my childhood room, the walls decorated colourfully with posters of my favourite movie characters and superheroes. There was a time when I looked up to these protagonists, when I couldn't wait to turn their age and become like them. The sad fact was, I outgrew them. I continued to age, and they didn't. Oh how the everlasting illusion of fiction can be cruel.

As I got older, I found other heroes. Racing drivers, football players, rock stars. People I admired and respected. There's something very human about admiration, noticing good qualities in others and trying to embody them. We need our heroes, they inspire, teach and motivate and they're often the only ones who can cut through the noise. It's true that we are all the people we admire. But we are also the writers we read, the music we sing. We are the films that inspire, the characters that live within. We are the artists and poets whose prose captivates our thoughts more deeply than we could ever explain. We are the dreams we pursue, the passions we embrace, the love we give, the kindness we receive. We are the influences of other influences, the thoughts of other thoughts. We are the collective spirit of all that touches our heart and souls, woven into the tapestry of each other. I saw it and I finally understood it. We've each got a part of each other.

Between these walls sat my everything. The first place I grew and changed. Yet, this was as far as my world reached when I was 8 or 9. This wasn't just a moment in time, it was a person. My thoughts ended abruptly as I was interrupted by the sound of footsteps. I rushed downstairs, shouting for the person to stop. There was no response, but as I ran back into the living room, I saw someone run out the back gate, where I followed swiftly.

65

CHAPTER 8

Through the gate, I moved forward, passing down a corridor of trees. I didn't get far, as a shadow of movement behind the wall of green caught my attention. Whoever it was, seemed to have taken a shortcut through. I did the same, pushing through the hedges until I reached the other side.

Stumbling out, I was surprised to find myself on a gravel path, surrounded by sharp hedges and trimmed flowers. A very well kept area, perhaps this was where the gardeners worked their magic? Up ahead in the distance was a greenhouse, a huge Victorian structure encased in white iron. I was close enough that I could see the lush greenery within, pressing up against the top of the glass.

Moving on through the garden, looking for signs of life, I was surprised to see a snake dart across the gravel in front of me. A strange coincidence, but it made me realise how much I identified with the snake's journey. Over the course of my life, I too had worn many skins: a curious child, awkward teenager, student and nurse. Each was its own form of change. Make no mistake, discarding old skin is painful. There's a certainty to old skin, an identity. I had worn mine for years, it made me feel safe and comfortable. But sometimes change is needed. In the case of a snake, if it can't shed its skin, it can go blind or even die. My new feelings now made sense, for when I discarded my old skin, I hadn't lost myself, I had discovered it.

Moving on through again, and I came across the entrance to the greenhouse. The doors beneath were swinging. Whoever it was, appeared to have gone inside. I approached with caution. As I got closer, I could hear running water. I looked at my arms, my burns had now begun to ache. I needed water, and I was curious, so I decided to enter.

The greenhouse was beautiful, filled ceiling to floor with deep long strands of green. A metal balcony, wrapped around the upper level with stairs at each end. I moved on through the green, around it and straight along the path to the centre where the fountain stood.

Perched over the fountain, I collected handfuls of water, which I held above me and let slip through my fingers, streaming over my face. The water spilled over the fountain, running, misting and splashing around me. I tended to my burns and cuts, washing them clean. All was quiet, until a gust of wind blew softly through the air above, carrying a hint of music. I looked around. Notes played slowly one after the other, then arpeggios, and finally chords. A peep through the bushes beside me showed a shadow of a pianist. His back arched, his hands forward, gracefully examining the keys as he played, his hands flinging themselves into the air, his fingers dancing, twirling. His manner confident, his skills controlled and admitted.

I scuttled back to my perch, leaning politely against the fountain. Other instruments began to occupy the air. Closing my eyes, I could feel the chords rising past my ears, bouncing off the walls and falling back down to earth. Faster and more frequent they became, until I was bathed in a constant flow of sound, and then, silence. A moment before the storm. Listen closely, the bow quivering above the strings, hands poised over keys, baton ready to slice the air. You can almost hear it, almost see it. As could I.

And then, it began. The bow kissed the strings, fingers politely danced and twirled upon the keys. Horns soared through the air, ricocheting off the glass walls. Notes burst above, showering me in a glittering rain of melodies.

With the sound swelling up around me, I moved quickly through the exotic plants and trees, across the paving stones, round past the arched glass corner, and up the spiral staircase. Halfway, and I paused to catch my breath, taking a moment to look at the plants below. They were swaying, moving, dancing with the music. Up the stairs again, moving gently across the balcony. Reaching out to the plants closest to me, my fingers interlocking with theirs. Not just touching but feeling. That was when I got to grinning, for I was at one with it all.

Continuing to traverse, the final crescendo pressing against my skin, seeping into my bones. Shamelessly, I not only let it wash over me, I let it wash through me. Deeper and deeper until I could no longer tell where the music ended, and I began.

For just a moment I balanced on the peak point of gratification that we all so desire. Intoxicated with art, flowing through me, restoring my ability to turn my thoughts into feelings, my feelings into words. Like all good things, it did not last. My enjoyable moment ended when the silence returned, pulling me back to the present.

Upon returning to the fountain and wiping my face clean. I caught sight of myself in the reflection of the water and was horrified to see that I was smiling. I moved forward through the shrubs, to where the pianist was sat. No one was there. Nothing, not even a piano as I had imagined. But in the corner sat a gramophone. I couldn't believe it. It all felt so real, the music, the emotions. My feelings were real, even if what I saw was not.

There I was, crouched beside the gramophone, listening to the prominent crackle of the disk as it skipped over the last groove. Suddenly, my vision went astonishingly dark and crows made their calls

on the balcony above. This was followed by an almighty bang of thunder which lifted me to my feet and out the door.
Staggering out, I found myself at the entrance to a hedge maze. The storm had finally caught up to me once again. I searched for an escape route, but the hedges surrounded me on all sides. I went back inside, to the other side of the greenhouse where I had first entered. It was locked. I tried the other door, that too was locked.

The fog moved in fast, snaking through the doors, amongst the plants and up to my knees. To be honest with you, I wasn't sure if it was fog, it behaved in such an odd manner, as if it had a mind of it's own. But that did not matter. I felt a sudden sense of urgency. The sky was getting darker, the world was fading away and I knew my time was coming to an end.

Running back into the greenhouse, down the path, around the fountain and finally up the stairs. Moving across the balcony, clambering up against the outer wall to try and find an open window. Eventually after a struggle with the stiff lock, I found one. Head popping out, I could see the hedge maze from above. Another perspective, a solution. Creativity often comes out of a striving frustration to achieve something. With eyes locked onto that image, tracing the way, I ran down the stairs again, across the floor and out the door.

The emerald green hedges surrounded me on all sides as I navigated the labyrinth of twists and turns. I took a couple of wrong turns on the way, but I persevered on through. I knew I had reached the centre when I came across the stone monument. Frantically, I moved around it, trying to find clues or an escape. On the far side a weathered iron door was nestled deep within its walls. Heart pounding, I threw it open to reveal only inky darkness within. This void was my only way out. Saying a silent prayer, I jumped weightlessly into an unfathomable shadow, leaving the fog behind.

CHAPTER 9

Weightlessness enveloped me as I plunged into darkness. The rushing of air, my only companion as I fell through the void. After what felt like an eternity, my feet struck solid ground. Darkness lay in front of me, pure black, nothing. But yet, I could see hope.

I steadied myself, palms up against cold stone, shuffling along as my eyes adjusted. I was in some kind of underground cave or tunnel, the walls wet and cold. I shuffled forward through the darkness, until a pinprick of light came into view. As I got closer, echoes of whispers seemed to follow me through the inky blackness. The voices grew louder, though the words remained indistinct.

Emerging into dim candle light, I found myself in a cavernous room. Jagged stalactites hung ominously from the ceiling, glistening with mineral deposits. An open archway in front of me, showed the room branched out into a walkway, to the right of which was some sort of underground river. From where I stood I could see two boats tethered to the side of the walkway.

Looking back up the corridor behind, I could already see the fog seeping down into the cave. I decided to press on. Through the arch I went, onto the platform and into the boat, soon kicking my heel against the stone platform. I didn't have much of a choice, but I hoped my decision would lead me to safety.

I had already begun to cast off, when a selection of limbs erupted from the tunnel and made for the end of the walkway. The two figures shouted, and I turned to see Mr Buttons and the young version of myself. They were hanging on to each other. I'm still unsure who was holding onto whom.

In a frantic scurry, I stopped the boat with my feet against the cave wall and turned back to them. After docking, I scrambled up to them, the boy running into my arms before I could open them.

"After all this, after all the time, all the pain: I'm so glad I looked for you." I said to him.

"I missed you." the boy replied.

"It's okay, we're here now." I said, wiping the tear from his cheek. He appeared to study me for a moment, looking at the burns and marks on my face.

"You've changed." he said.

"We've all changed," I replied, "and we will continue to change. That's what life is all about. We spend our lives seeking comfort, and when we find it, we bury ourselves deep within it. But on the odd occasion, when all is quiet, something will come along that'll rip us out of the ground and throw us into the unknown. A place where everything means nothing, nothing means everything and where comforts cease to be. It's hard, there's no denying that, but remember, often the hardest and most unexpected situations can encourage the best type of change, growth."

I turned to Mr Buttons, a glimpse of tears in his eyes. I knew by his reaction that he too saw my bruises, burns and cuts.

"My dear boy." he said.

"Please, don't worry about me." I replied. "These wounds will heal, my bruises will fade and I'll be okay. That's the important thing. I'll be okay."

He smiled at me, "There is one change everyone seems to be scared of: ageing. We all wish we could grow older without negative challenges or changes. The aching joints, thinning hair, sagging skin.

But every one of those changes tells a story and I think there's something beautiful in that."

"My scars are like that," I replied, "just some souvenirs I earned along the way."

Mr Buttons flicked his cane up into the air, catching it as it flew up towards him and began to examine the handle. "True, but unfortunately getting old isn't seen in the same way. I just wish people could see ageing for what it is; experience, authenticity and depth. It is not a sign of decline or loss, it's quite the opposite. Too many friends of mine never had the opportunity to grow old. It's a privilege to age, don't you forget it."

"It's a privilege to be here," I replied, "thank you."

After placing his cane against the wall, he carefully moved back towards me. My arm was already held out ready to shake his hand. He took hold of my fingers and pulled me towards him, wrapping himself around me. I did the same, holding onto him tightly, after all how could I not love someone who saw all forms of beauty?

"Thank you." I whispered into his ear.

"No, thank you." he replied. "Thank you."

I gestured for the boy to come and join us and we all held each other for a moment. By this time the fog had begun to snake around us, the worlds colours fading.

The boy noticed it first and looked up at us. "You must go." he said. "You must go."

Almost immediately after he said that, the sound of a clock striking filled the air. The ground seemed to shake, continuing long after the sound was gone. Mr Buttons picked up his cane and moved towards the end of the walkway, "I must go." he said.

"Where are you going?" I asked.

"Home." he replied, getting into one of the boats. "I suggest you do the same."

I looked at the boy. "He's right," he said, "you must go. I belong here, I'll be okay."

Into the other boat I went. Just before we cast off Mr Buttons turned to me, placing his hand on my shoulder. "If your memory serves you well, we're going to meet again." he said.

"I believe that." I replied.

The fog was thick now, the air thick enough to swallow. Both ends of the river were obscured. As we set off on our separate ways, I watched as Mr Buttons became nothing but a silhouette.

My attention then turned to the boy. He wiped his sleeve over his eyes. How sad he looked. I could do nothing but watch as he got smaller and smaller. As the fog engulfed me, his eyes were the last thing I saw. Shiny pupils that reflected the light, surrounded by a shade of pink.

I was engulfed by the fog, everything appearing to turn a bright white. The boat I was in seemed to vanish from beneath me. Once again, only for a second or two, I was flying.

CHAPTER 10

It was the falling sensation that brought me back. When I opened my eyes, the room was unbearably bright. Sunlight poured through the window, casting over every object with an uncomfortable sharpness. Nurses and doctors proceeded to float into the room, nodding and mumbling as they congregated at my feet. I watched and noted their movements and mannerisms precisely as I struggled to believe they were real.

My consciousness seemed to have lacked the practice of being used. Despite being under for nearly four weeks, the only thing I wanted to do was go back to sleep. Keeping my eyes open was exhausting, every time I slipped back under the doctors and nurses kept pulling me up and out. My barely functioning mind, stretched in all directions. I was asked the "do you know your name?", "what year are we in?" questions. It was hard to make sense of my replies as everything came out in such a jumbled mess. My mouth felt like it was filled with dry rags, my throat bruised from the breathing tube.

Doctors couldn't believe I survived. My legs were crushed in the accident, my lungs collapsed and I suffered an extensive brain injury. I spent almost a month bedridden and required intense therapy, both physio and occupational. I had to learn how to walk again, how to use the toilet, how to look after myself. I then spent an extra two months at a live-in rehabilitation centre, and another four months in outpatient care.

Before all this, I was constantly calculating, thinking I was wasting my 'good' years. Then the accident happened, and suddenly, all the things I'd been worrying about disappeared. I found out how fragile life is, and learned that worrying about tomorrow's problems does nothing but ruin todays peace.

Due to my injuries, I couldn't move around as I used to, so I had to buy a cane to walk with. I ended up getting a custom cane made, a replica of Mr Buttons. Dark oak, with a silver snake shaped handle. A reminder, something I could carry with me and be proud of.

In the months and years after, I engrossed myself in life and intoxicated myself with art. I found joy in gardening, I learned how to play the piano, quit my job and pursued my dreams as best as I could. With some adaptations, I managed to travel the world and I wrote about my experience as you see before you, an achievement I am most proud of.

I know my experience may be ridiculed, my words may be judged, but it doesn't change the fact they are mine and this is my story. Art may be criticised, mocked and burned, but it can never be ignored. I'm lucky really, you don't realise how easily death can come for you until you've sat at that doorstep and lived to tell the tale.

Even as my story draws to a close, I will still be here. The immortality of art can be cruel, but it can also be wonderful. Fleeting moments, emotions and perspectives, captured and preserved for all to see and understand. So much beauty lies in creation. Those inherent attempts to express how we truly feel. Opening ourselves to the world, letting others in. Showing others that they are seen and acknowledged. A sense of belonging. A sense of being. There is nothing more important.

I don't pretend to understand the mysteries of life, there are still lots of unanswered questions and things to discover, but isn't that the fun of it? The mystery? Even here, maybe I'm wrong about all this.

After all, death is the only true certainty we have in life. We're all going to die: me, you, everyone. That is just a fact. It's unfortunate that while we've evolved so much, we're still so dismissive of death, what comes next. The idea of not knowing cripples many of us. We prefer to cling to the idea of knowledge. What things are, what things mean, who we are and why we're here. But the worst thing one can do is avoid the idea of death. It's not that death should be invited or desired, but it should be respected. Life is change, death is simply part of that change and there is no evolution or growth without it.

I know death is sad, but that sadness is a sign of care, a sign of love.

Although we're all destined to become stories, right now, we still have the power to change how our story ends. You can't go back and change the past, but you can start where you are and change the ending. Every moment is an opportunity, it's never too late to start a new chapter. It's often not easy, there's no denying that. Sometimes you'll wish you could skip pages, delete chapters and start all over. But mistakes are how we learn. It's what makes us human, and there's nothing more poetic than being human.

Life is simply the long undressing for the dark endless night. Learn to embrace it because of the finality of death, not drift through it due to its inevitability. Life doesn't come with a trial period, time doesn't come with a money back guarantee. Time isn't a currency. You can't save it, you can't store it, and the rich certainly don't have more of it. Time is a problem, a solution, a gift and a curse. It's everything we have and don't. The passage of time is somewhat of an illusion, and like an illusion, it depends on how you view it. But one thing is for certain: we must learn to enjoy what we have of it. So learn to be brave, learn to proceed without certainty. Open yourself up to new experiences, meet people, experience new cultures, and learn from your mistakes. Don't let your curiosity die of age, never lose your sense of wonder. Always strive toward the truth, no matter how frightening or unpleasant it may be. We're only here for a short while. We shouldn't waste our time claiming we know the answers to the things we don't, nor should we fear what we don't know. We must try and understand and learn from each other.

Try and live the life you want to live. Intoxicate yourself with art, whether it be literature, sculpture, cinema, theatre or music. Express yourself, experiment, create, fail and try again. Learn to love the silence between notes, the space between words. Of course, on some days, just being here is enough. That's okay. Life is meant to be lived, not constantly figured out. You are not a problem that needs solving. Breathe, rest, work and play. All things in moderation.

Ignore those who bully and mock. You are under no obligation to prove anything to anyone but yourself. Only you know what you've been through, how far you've come, how much you've grown.

You may not believe it, but we're all trying to figure out the same thing in life. There are over 8 billion people in the world, people like you and I, getting on with their lives. We're all pretty much the same. You, me, your idols. All born on the same earth, with more or less the same insides. Despite what you may think, no one is in charge of the world, and no one really knows how it all works, only that it does, so long as each group does what it's meant to be doing.

Headlines and newspapers like to make out that we live in a world full of hatred and violence, but I don't think that's true. I could spend hours going into detail about every exception, but that's not the point. The point is, if you pay close attention, in almost every instance of our lives you'll find that love is all around us. Small, subtle acts of kindness, strangers standing up to let you get to your seat at the theatre. Holding open the door and smiling, reaching for something high on a shelf. Love that is often too quiet to notice, too gentle to recognise. But it's still love.

The truth is, most of us don't want to harm each other. We just want the bus to turn up on time, and to thank the driver as we get off. To wave and smile at the postie as we pass him in the street, and for our friends to get home safely after a night out.

We're simple creatures really, and I know we've grown far from the foresters and hunter-gatherers we once were, but after all that time, to know that love and kindness are still our default states of being, well I think that's quite something.

Whenever I feel sad, I look for those little bits of love. The calm and quiet types. If you miss them, as I often do, don't feel bad. Most of us don't pay attention to the sea when it is calm.

If you're feeling like I was, please don't be harsh on yourself. You're the one who picks yourself up from the floor, washes, clothes, feeds yourself, even on your darkest days. You are a miracle, you are enough. Be kind to yourself. Close each chapter with love and remember, the sun will rise again.

Oh, and I did see Mr Buttons again. Years later, on the anniversary of my accident, I was walking alone through a field of wild flowers and I came across a stream bordered by some lovely yellow blossoms, Cotula Coronopifolia they were called, also known as brass buttons or yellow buttons. I followed them, watching as the stream trickled into a large pond. As I got closer and stared down into the water, I noticed Mr Buttons reflection looking back at me.

"I spent a lifetime looking for you, and now I will spend a lifetime living for you." I muttered with a grin.

The man in the reflection was already smiling back.

Me, myself and I.
The dream to end all dreams.
By Jonathan (Mr Buttons)

<u>ACKNOWLEDGEMENTS</u>

To my wonderful beta readers, Dave Harrison, Shelby Eagleson and Aurelio Muraca. I can't thank you enough for your enthusiasm and wonderful feedback.

Thank you to all the people who gave up their time to support and mentor me. Who believed in me when I didn't believe in myself, who encouraged me to continue and insisted I could do it. Your kindness continues to astound me. I am so lucky to be surrounded by so many wonderful people.

INSPIRATIONS

<u>Places:</u>
Sanssouci Park, Potsdam, Germany
Portmeirion, Penrhyndeudraeth, Wales
Tupgill Park, Leyburn, England
Stourhead, Warminster, England
Mother Shipton's Cave, Knaresborough, England
Sherberton West Dart Stepping Stones, Dartmoor, England

<u>Books:</u>
'The Stranger' by Albert Camus
'Siddhartha' by Hermann Hesse
'The Little Prince' by Antoine de Saint-Exupery
'Being There' by Jerzy Kosiński
'Bridge to Terabithia' by Katherine Paterson
'The Secret' by Rhonda Byrne
'Autobiography of a Yogi' by Paramahansa Yogananda
'Be Here Now' by Ram Dass
'The Prophet' by Kahlil Gibran

<u>Films/Programmes:</u>
The Prisoner (1967)
Last Night In Soho (2021)
What Dreams May Come (1998)
Lonely Bones (2009)
Alice in Wonderland (1966)
The Seventh Seal (1957)
Afterlife (2019)
Wings of Fame (1990)

Man of La Mancha (1972)
The Hourglass Sanatorium (1973)
Valerie And Her Week Of Wonders (1970)
Midnight Mass (2021)
The Meaning of Life (1983)
Monty Python's Meaning of Life (1983)
Time Bandits (1981)
Ways of Seeing (1972)

<u>Songs:</u>
'Routine Day' by Klaatu
'The Galaxy Song' by Eric Idle
'Ink Pot Eyes' by Nick Garrie

People:
Ram Dass - "Be Here Now", "We're all just walking each other home."

Viktor E. Frankl - "The meaning of life is to give life meaning."

Diane Ackerman - "Don't just live the length of your life, live the width of it as well."

Earl Nightingale – "Don't let the fear of the time it will take to accomplish something stand in the way of your doing it. The time will pass anyway; we might just as well put that passing time to the best possible use."

Roy T. Bennett - "The past is a place of reference, not a place of residence; the past is a place of learning, not a place of living."

Ziad K. Abdelnour - "Life is like a camera. Focus on what's important. Capture the good times. And if things don't work out, just take another shot."

C.S. Lewis – "I sat with my anger long enough until she told me her real name was grief."

Mark Twain - "I do not fear death. I had been dead for billions and billions of years before I was born, and had not suffered the slightest inconvenience from it."

Dale Wasserman (Man of La Mancha) - "I have lived nearly fifty years, and I have seen life as it is. Pain, misery, hunger ... cruelty beyond belief. I have heard the singing from taverns and the moans from bundles of filth on the streets. I have been a soldier and seen my comrades fall in battle ... or die more slowly under the lash in Africa. I have held them in my arms at the final moment. These were men who saw life as it is, yet they died despairing. No glory, no gallant last words ... only their eyes filled with confusion, whimpering the question, "Why?" I do not think they asked why they were dying, but why they had lived. When life itself seems lunatic, who knows where madness lies? Perhaps to be too practical is madness. To surrender dreams — this may be madness. To seek treasure where there is only trash. Too much sanity may be madness — and maddest of all: to see life as it is, and not as it should be!"

Richard Brooks (Lord Jim) - "I've been a so-called coward and a so-called hero and there's not the thickness of a sheet of paper between them. Maybe cowards and heroes are just ordinary men who, for a split second, do something out of the ordinary."

Sylvia Plath - "The floor seemed wonderfully solid. It was comforting to know I had fallen and could fall no farther."

Henry David Thoreau – "The question is not what you look at that matters, but what you see."

Jorge Luis Borges - "I am not sure that I exist, actually. I am all the writers that I have read, all the people that I have met, all the women that I have loved; all the cities I have visited."